Y0-BVF-931

Mother Goose
NURSERY RHYMES

Compiled by Emma Bailey
Illustrated by Loretta Krupinski

GALLERY BOOKS
An Imprint of W. H. Smith Publishers Inc.
112 Madison Avenue
New York City 10016

HUMPTY DUMPTY

Humpty Dumpty sat on a wall,
Humpty Dumpty had a great fall;
All the king's horses
And all the king's men
Couldn't put Humpty Dumpty
Together again.

HEY, DIDDLE DIDDLE!

Hey diddle, diddle,
The cat and the fiddle,
The cow jumped over the moon.
The little dog laughed
To see such sport,
And the dish ran away with the spoon.

LITTLE BOY BLUE

Little Boy Blue, come blow your horn;
The sheep's in the meadow, the cow's in the corn.
Where is the boy who looks after the sheep?
He's under the haystack fast asleep!

JACK AND JILL

Jack and Jill went up the hill
To fetch a pail of water;
Jack fell down and broke his crown,
And Jill came tumbling after.

MARY, MARY QUITE CONTRARY

Mary, Mary quite contrary,
How does your garden grow?
With silver bells and cockle-shells
And pretty maids all in a row.

BAA, BAA BLACK SHEEP

Baa, baa, black sheep,
Have you any wool?
Yes Sir, yes Sir,
Three bags full.
One for my master,
One for my dame,
And one for the little boy
Who lives down the lane.

DIDDLE, DIDDLE DUMPLING

Diddle, diddle dumpling, my son John
Went to bed with his trousers on,
One shoe off, and one shoe on,
Diddle, diddle dumpling, my son John.

LITTLE MISS MUFFET

Little Miss Muffet sat on a tuffet,
Eating some curds and whey;
Along came a spider
And sat down beside her,
And frightened Miss Muffet away.

ONE, TWO BUCKLE MY SHOE

One, Two — buckle my shoe;

Three, Four — knock at the door;

Five, Six — pick up sticks;

Seven, Eight — lay them straight;

Nine, Ten — a big fat hen.

OLD KING COLE

Old King Cole was a merry old soul,
And a merry old soul was he.
He called for his pipe,
And he called for his drum,
And he called for his fiddlers three.

THE QUEEN OF HEARTS

The Queen of Hearts,
She made some tarts
All on a summer's day.
The Knave of Hearts,
He stole those tarts,
And took them clean away.

LITTLE BO-PEEP

Little Bo-Peep has lost her sheep,
And can't tell where to find them.
Leave them alone, and they'll come home,
Wagging their tails behind them.

HICKORY, DICKORY, DOCK

Hickory, dickory, dock,
The mouse ran up the clock;
The clock struck one,
The mouse ran down,
Hickory, dickory, dock.

THE STAR

Twinkle, twinkle, little star,
How I wonder what you are,
Up above the world so high
Like a diamond in the sky.